Murder
at St. Mark's

Priscilla Baker

Cover Design by http://www.StunningBookCovers.com

For Zach

Chapter 1

"Coming through! Hot!" a loud voice called out.

Lucy Moretti stopped moving and watched as a server carrying a large tray of entrees pushed through the swinging door out into the dining room. As he vanished from view, she started walking again, hoping to sneak through the kitchen and back to her office without being noticed.

"Boss, got a sec?" one of the line cooks called out to Lucy as she moved behind him.

"Sure, what's up?" she asked.

"Almost out of the polenta side that's being served with the special," he called back, "What do you want us to use next?"

"Gotta ask Chef, you know that. I'll send her over," Lucy replied. With that, she kept walking.

The executive chef, Alison Pope, was a recent hire and the staff were taking their time getting used to her. Even with training at Johnson & Wales and years at various restaurants up and down the East Coast, including a Michelin starred restaurant in New York City, Alison had to earn her place at the head of Lucy's culinary team. Lucy knew it had been a tough transition for Ally, from sous chef in New York to executive chef here. But really, she had been doing a great job. And a question about a side dish was definitely in her wheelhouse.

Lucy finally reached the office and found Alison there, flipping through her recipe binders.

"Hey, Ally, they're almost out of the polenta side. Raul needs to know what you want to do next."

"On it," Ally replied. She stood up and shrugged her chef coat back on before leaving the office, buttoning it up as she went. Lucy sighed and sank into her chair, reaching for the cup of coffee she'd set down earlier next to her computer. Of course, by now it was cold.

She looked up at the picture of herself and Alison at their college graduation, hanging above her computer, and smiled, remembering when they thought that exams and cooking classes were hard. Their joy practically shone out of the photograph, Lucy's dark hair and Ally's blonde both standing out against the green grass. The picture had been taken the first year they lived together, randomly assigned as roommates. Ally was working her way through the culinary program, and Lucy was earning her degree in hospitality management so she could take over the family business. They had eaten better than most college students during those years, with Ally constantly bringing home leftovers and failed experiments from class. Lucy could cook, coming from a family of restaurant owners, but her skills were nothing compared to Ally's.

After four years of sharing a room, and meals every night, Lucy and Ally were best friends. After graduation, they had gone their separate ways, Ally to Charleston, South Carolina to try to land a job, and Lucy back to Boston to start her second round of schooling at Alba, the restaurant her grandparents had started, which at the time was being run by her father.

Lucy had really been in training to take over Alba for most of her life, but she moved into new gear once she graduated. Moving back home meant living in her old room in the apartment over the restaurant. She had waited tables at Alba before college, but now took on more serving and bartending shifts than ever before, in addition to taking on some of her father's tasks. Within five years of graduation, she had taken over the front of house operations and was working closely with Jackson, the previous chef, who had worked at the restaurant longer than she had been alive. Lucy could still remember sitting in this very office with him while he worked on menus and teased the cooks about their mistakes. He had retired years ago, and now was filling his time with fishing down in the Florida Keys. In the years since Jackson had retired, Lucy's father hired a few different head chefs, none lasting longer than a year. But now, Lucy and Ally were finally working together, living their college dream, and things were looking up.

Lucy glanced up from her reverie as Ally returned to the office.

"All taken care of…we're switching to sautéed green beans with shaved red peppers. That was meant to be the side dish for tomorrow's special, the cod, but I'll head over to the farmer's market in the morning and see what I can get to replace it."

"Sure, whatever works," Lucy responded, "it's your call." She turned to her computer, trying to remember what she was working on in the first place. *Labor*, she remembered. She was hoping to find something extra in her labor budget to bring on another dishwasher over the summer. With business picking up, they needed one.

The time passed quickly, and before she knew it an hour had passed and Lucy had to get up and stretch her legs. She strolled through the kitchen, intending to head out to the dining room.

Where's Alberto? Lucy thought, noticing that one of her line cooks wasn't at his station. She headed out to the alley behind the restaurant where the staff liked to sneak off to take smoke breaks. A tell-tale orange light flickered across the alley, but it was too dark for Lucy to see who was holding the cigarette. Taking a chance, she called out, "Alberto!"

On the other side of the alley the light jumped and dropped to the ground, where it was quickly put out by someone's shoe.

"Coming, boss," rose a deep, guilty voice out of the darkness.

"I know the weather is finally warming up outside, but we need you in here! It will still be nice out on your day off, I promise," Lucy called out. She went back inside, letting the door close behind her. Without having to look, she knew that Alberto would follow. Lucy let herself smile a moment later as she heard the door open again behind her, signalling Alberto's return to work.

The rest of the night passed in a blur until suddenly it was after midnight and the servers were crowding around her, ready to turn over their receipts and cash sales for the night, leaving Lucy to reconcile the numbers and check the math.

Just as quickly as the employees had appeared, they all vanished, joking and shouting as they pushed down the stairs to the locker room where they would change before disappearing into the night. Lucy tried to organize and count all the slips of paper that had been pushed into her hands, checking to see if all of her servers had been in the group. They were young and energetic, and the customers loved them, but collectively, they could definitely be a handful for her.

There was a knock on the door frame and Lucy looked up to see Donovan Fagan, another server, standing in the entrance. "Hey, Lucy, just dropping off my sales," he said as he handed her the slip.

"Hey, Donovan, thanks. How was it out there?" Lucy asked. Donovan was only in his thirties, but had been at the restaurant since he was a teenager. When he was scheduled to work, Lucy knew that she didn't have to worry about the servers at all. Donovan could always keep them in line, and they looked up to him.

"Things went pretty smoothly. Customers were happy, servers were happy, couldn't have asked for anything more," he said, slouching against the door frame as he spoke.

"Listen, Lucy," he continued. "I may have to take a few days off, coming up. Get some time away. Is that okay?" he asked.

"Sure thing, Donovan. Just make sure you let me know exactly when ahead of time. We'll just have to figure out how to get by without you!" Lucy responded, smiling. "And thanks for bringing by your sales. Now get out of here! I'll see you tomorrow." Lucy turned back to the spreadsheet on her computer, and started to work.

Chapter 2

The following morning, Lucy startled awake at the sound of pounding on the door to her small apartment above Alba. She groaned and rolled over, hoping whoever it was would go away. She glanced at the clock on her night table and winced when she saw it was only quarter to ten in the morning. Late for the rest of the world, but awfully early when you had been at work closing a restaurant until four a.m. the night before.

The noise stopped briefly while the pounder spoke, "I need you to open the door. This is Officer Fitz from the Boston Police Department."

Damn, Lucy thought, *I guess that means I really have to get up.* She climbed out of bed and grabbed the robe hanging on the back of her door, wrapping it around herself. She hurried out of the bedroom and across the living room to the front door, smoothing her dark curly hair back into a ponytail as she went. Just as she reached it, she pivoted, taking a few steps to the left and closing the door to the second bedroom next to hers. It has been her childhood bedroom, but these days it functioned as a storage unit for the restaurant. Whoever was knocking certainly didn't need to see that mess.

She reached the front door just as the pounding resumed, opening it while the police officer's fist was still in the air.

On the other side of the door, standing on her little balcony raised up above the alleyway behind the restaurant, was a man wearing a Boston Police Department uniform. He was a little taller than she was and was clutching a handful of papers. He had light brown hair, and green eyes that seemed to sparkle in the morning light.

"Good morning ma'am, I'm sorry to disturb you. My name is Officer Fitz of the BPD and I need to speak to you regarding an incident in the neighborhood last night. Are you the owner of the restaurant below, Lucy..." he trailed off, shuffling through his papers.

"Moretti," Lucy answered, baffled as to why he was at her door in the first place. *An incident in the neighborhood? What on earth does that mean?* she wondered. Sure, there was the occasional fight or burglary, but the cops had never shown up at her door before.

"Yes ma'am, Lucy Moretti. Are you the owner of Alba?" As he spoke, he glanced past her into the apartment, which was a disaster.

"Yes, sir. I own and manage Alba. What can I help you with?" Lucy moved a little in the doorway, hoping to block the pile of laundry she knew was just behind on her the other side of the room. Living alone, it was easy to lose control of the laundry situation.

"Do you employ a Donovan Fagan in the restaurant?" The officer looked straight ahead, not making eye contact.

"Yes, Officer, I do. I've known him for years. What's the problem?"

The officer sighed, finally making eye contact with Lucy. "Ma'am, I regret to inform you that Mr. Fagan's body was discovered this morning in the courtyard of St. Mark's Church over on Hanover Street. We suspect foul play."

Lucy gasped, feeling like someone had punched her in the gut. She slouched forward and Officer Fitz put a steadying hand on her arm. "Ma'am, would you like to sit down?" Without waiting for an answer, he guided her back inside the small apartment to the couch that was visible from the doorway. They sat down and he looked at her expectantly, waiting for a response.

Lucy gathered her strength and looked up at him—even sitting down he was tall. "What happened? Foul play? What does that even mean?" she quizzed the officer.

Officer Fitz started to answer, "Ma'am…"

Lucy held up a hand and cut him off. "Please, not ma'am. Just call me Lucy."

"Okay, Lucy. Mr. Fagan was found early this morning in the courtyard at St. Mark's. He was found by the cleaning lady who goes in before services begin. He was declared deceased on the spot."

"But...how?" Lucy started to interrupt again, but this time it was Officer Fitz who held up his hand and continued to speak.

"He was stabbed. With a steak knife. Unfortunately, it has the Alba logo on the handle. Are you familiar with the type of knife I'm describing?" He paused and looked at her.

Lucy felt the blood rush to her head. *A steak knife, with the Alba logo on the handle?* That was what they used in the restaurant downstairs. She owned hundreds of them. But how did one get out of the restaurant, let alone stab one of her employees at the church down the street?

She voiced the question out loud, "Yes, I know exactly what you're describing. But how did one of my knives end up being used to stab one of my servers? You still haven't told me what happened!" Her voice rose in frustration.

"Ma'am—Lucy—this is an ongoing investigation. We don't have any answers as to what happened at this moment. I do need to ask you another question. Do you have any contact information for a next of kin for Mr. Donovan? We'd like to inform his family, if possible." Officer Fitz seemed to relax slightly as he came to the point of his visit, and he leaned back into the couch.

"Of course...I know he had an aunt, I think. His parents passed quite a while ago. Let me check...maybe in his employee file in my office downstairs. If you can just wait a moment..." she trailed off and looked at the officer, hoping he would protest so she didn't have to go all the way down to the restaurant this early. He stayed silent and looked at her expectantly.

Lucy rose and slipped on the pair of shoes next to the door as she grabbed her keys from an eye hook on the wall her father had installed decades ago. Officer Fitz jumped up and pulled wide the front door to the apartment, gesturing for her to exit first. She stepped out on to her little porch and shivered, pulling her robe closer as the cool ocean breeze cut through her pajama pants. They were a few blocks away from the water, but still close enough to experience the cool sea air. She walked down the rickety wooden stairs and stopped at the bottom, where the back door to the restaurant was. She unlocked the door and stepped back, mirroring Officer Fitz's gesture for him to enter first. She reached past him as he did and flipped on the lights, revealing the industrial dish room that sat just inside the back door.

Lucy led the way through the kitchen, past the stainless steel counters and tables gleaming in the dark to the door to her office, which she unlocked with yet another key.

"Geez, how many keys does it take to get into this place?" Officer Fitz seemed to be attempting to make a joke, but it was impossible for Lucy to tell. She responded with a tight smile instead of an answer.

Once inside her office, Lucy sank down in her chair and gestured for Officer Fitz to take Alison's chair next to her. They shared one long desk pushed against the back wall of the office, with shelves above it. She opened one of the filing cabinets behind her and sorted through it, looking for the file with Donovan's name on it.

While she looked, Officer Fitz glanced back at the kitchen, taking it in. "If you don't mind my saying so, you seem awfully young to own a restaurant like this," he commented.

"Actually, I do mind" Lucy responded, still flipping through the files. "I don't see how my age is relevant at all. Alba is one of the most successful and longest-lasting restaurants in the area."

"I'm sorry," the officer apologized, "I didn't mean to offend you. I was just wondering how you were able to start your own restaurant. Just making small talk is all."

"No, it's okay." Lucy softened, regretting her hot-headed response. "I actually didn't start it. My grandparents were born in Italy and came to Boston in 1934. A few years later, just before the Second World War, they started the restaurant. They ran it for years, until the mid-eighties when my father took over. He and my mom ran it until three years ago, when they retired and I took over. They're living it up in Arizona these days. The restaurant is the family legacy." As she spoke, Lucy finally located Donovan's file and pulled it from the drawer.

"That's amazing. I wish I had something so tangible to show why my family came to America. My grandparents had a very different story," Officer Fitz mused. "Where did the name come from?' he asked.

"Well, it's a little convoluted. When my grandparents came here, and opened the restaurant with the war raging back in their country, they realized how lucky they were. 'Alba' means dawn in Italian, or at least something like it. So, my grandparents named the restaurant after their new beginning, in a new country."

"That's really sweet," Officer Fitz answered, as Lucy removed Donovan's file from the drawer and opened it so she and the officer could read together.

The file still had his original application in it, from over fifteen years ago, with her father's handwriting across the top. 'Hired,' it read in his big block writing. Lucy had still been a child when Donovan started working, spending her nights with her parents in the office they were now sitting in.

She handed the file to Officer Fitz but could tell right away it wouldn't be helpful; Donovan had drawn an 'X' through the section for a relative's information. Her father had always included it on the application after the time a server had collapsed in the kitchen back in the eighties.

"This is no help at all. Did he ever mention where the aunt might live?" Officer Fitz asked as he leafed through the old application.

"Honestly, no. I want to say she was his father's sister, though, so there's a chance her last name could still be Fagan. I think she was out of state, possibly up in Vermont? I know he would travel to see her, at least a few hours away." Lucy paused. "Do you mind if I make a cup of coffee?" she asked, starting to get up.

"Of course not," he answered, still reading. "Is it possible to get one myself? It was an early start this morning."

"Sure. Cream or sugar?" Lucy asked.

"Yes, cream, no sugar, thank you."

Lucy pushed through the swinging door and down past the line of burners that turned out hundreds of meals per night. It was always strange being in the kitchen so early, when no one else was there. At night, it was so loud and hot that it was tough to even think, but in the morning it was cool and quiet and dark. Lucy walked through the door to the first section of the dining room. It was broken up into three different areas—Lucy's grandparents had designed it that way to keep the place feeling cozy. She headed into the second dining room, where the bar was located. There was the espresso machine the customers loved. Lucy and her employees certainly took advantage of it as well.

Lucy turned the machine on and waited for it to warm up, listening to the quiet *whir* as she stared out the window. She couldn't believe it, Donovan was dead. *How? And how on earth had one of her knives ended up killing him?*

A siren broke into her thoughts as a black and white squad car drove down Salem Street and past the restaurant windows. *Is that related to Donovan? Is his body still at the church on the next street over?* She shuddered at the thought.

The machine finally beeped, indicating it was ready. She grabbed two of the disposable cups from under the counter and brewed the coffee into them. Her customers received their espresso and coffee in white china cups, but Lucy kept disposable ones underneath the bar for her staff. They preferred it anyway, since they could take the coffee with them when they left at the end of the night.

She grabbed the cups and made her way back to the office, where Officer Fitz was waiting for her, leaning against the door jamb.

"Listen, Lucy, I have to ask. Do you know how Mr. Fagan ended up being stabbed with a knife from your restaurant?" He looked directly at her as he took the coffee from her.

"Officer Fitz, I honestly have no idea. He could have taken it with him, I suppose? I don't know why he would, though." She blew on the coffee, and swirled it around in the cup, trying to cool it off.

"Is it possible someone here had a problem with him? Could another of the employees have followed him last night? Maybe a dispute over...tips or something?"

"Officer, no. My employees don't squabble over tips. Most of them have worked here for at least a decade, if not two. Besides, the tips go through me. The servers don't share among themselves, I take the tip out for the kitchen and add it on to everyone's paychecks myself." Lucy felt her voice getting louder as she spoke. "Besides, I've known most of these people since I was a teenager. Not one of them is capable of such a...such an awful thing."

"Okay, okay, I believe you!" Officer Fitz raised his hands in mock defeat, sloshing his coffee over the rim of the cup. He slurped the spilled coffee off his hand and smiled at her. "Listen, I really do believe you. But the fact is, a man is dead and I have to find out why. And I know you knew him well, and I'm sorry to have to put you through this."

He leaned against the door jamb again, still smiling at her. Lucy didn't like how comfortable he looked, drinking coffee and relaxing in her office.

Something occurred to Lucy. "Officer Fitz, all of my employees have lockers downstairs in the basement. There might be something in there that could point you in the right direction to contact his family. Would you like to go downstairs and check?" she offered.

"Yes, definitely. That could be really helpful. Can we go right now?" he asked.

"Follow me." Lucy pivoted into the stairwell directly next to the office door. She went down the stairs, flicking the light switch at the top as she went. She didn't check behind her to see if the officer was following.

They reached the bottom of the stairs where Lucy flicked the last light switch, illuminating the entire room. In front of them, across the room, was a bank of lockers that Lucy's father had purchased from a

Catholic school that was shutting down back in the nineties. To the left was the stone foundation of the building, blank except for a small window high up in the center that opened into the street. Off to the right was another doorway that led to the wine cellar.

Lucy crossed the flagstone floor, Officer Fitz close behind. "Do you know which is his locker?" the officer asked.

"Of course, Officer Fitz. You seem to keep forgetting the fact that most of these people have been here since my father ran the restaurant. Some of them longer than I've been alive. Things don't change too often around here."

Lucy reached the lockers and immediately pinpointed the larger one in the middle, with 'Donny' scrawled on it in permanent marker. Someone had written it years ago; Lucy didn't even know who. She opened the locker with one hand and stepped back so Officer Fitz could see inside.

"No locks? Interesting," he observed as he peered inside.

"Officer, yet again, no secrets around here. My employees are closer to siblings than to coworkers. They don't lock their lockers." Lucy shook her head at the officer's unwillingness to accept what she was saying.

The locker was almost empty. A pair of dress shoes, well worn, sat on the bottom shelf, with a something tucked behind them. It was a bright blue and purple ball cap. It had a logo on it, a baseball with two bats crossed behind it and a baseball player's helmet perched jauntily on the ball. On the back, where the hat was adjustable, the words 'Redmond, MA' were embroidered.

Redmond? Interesting, Lucy thought. Redmond was a town south of Boston, in an area called the South Shore, famous for its beaches and seafood.

"Damn," muttered the officer as he used the tip of his pen to move the hat and shoes around. "Nothing in here that will help."

He straightened and turned back towards the stairs. "Oh well," he said, "Thank you for bringing me down here, I really appreciate it."

They started back up the stairs together. As they reached the top, Lucy started to speak.

"Officer, is there anything else I can help you with? I'd like to get dressed and get started with my day. I have to figure out how to tell my staff that Donovan is dead, and I have to find someone to cover his shift tonight. In fact, I guess I have to get someone to cover all of his shifts." *That probably sounded a little callous*, Lucy thought. *Oh well. I'll never see this guy again.*

"That'll be it for now, ma'am. Thank you very much for the assistance. We'll try to get in touch with his aunt. If needed, is there a good number I can reach you at?" the officer asked.

Lucy stepped into the office and grabbed one of her business cards from her desk. "Here you are, Officer. Email, phone, everything is on there. You also know where I live." She handed over the card and crossed her arms, waiting for him to leave.

"Thanks very much. Have a good day. I'll be in touch regarding any developments." With that, Officer Fitz headed towards the back door where they had entered, dropping his now-empty coffee cup in one of the trash barrels in the dishroom.

Lucy sighed and locked up the door to her office again. She waited until the officer had left before heading out the back door herself and up to her apartment.

She sat back down on the couch and sighed. *Donovan, dead? What do I even do?* she wondered.

Lucy picked up the phone and dialed, tapping her fingers against her pajama-clad thigh while it rang.

Finally, an answer on the other end. She spoke, "Ally? I need you to come over."

Chapter 3

By five o'clock, the dinner service was starting to pick up. Lucy and Ally had made the announcement earlier, before the restaurant opened. They gathered all the staff in the dining room, and broke the news while the staff ate together. Every mid-afternoon, before the restaurant opened, Ally pulled together a meal for the staff, and they all ate out in the dining room. It was a great way for the staff to bond and keep close, and it was also a great time to make announcements. Usually, it was reminders about using the time clock and remembering to scrape the crumbs off of tables between courses, but today the announcement about Donovan was dark. The staff had reacted with gasps and tears, but as Lucy spoke to them, she couldn't help but remember Officer Fitz's words. Did anyone look like they weren't surprised by the news? She hated that he had forced her to wonder such awful things about her staff.

Now that the restaurant was open, Lucy's mind was caught in thoughts of Donovan's death. She was standing behind the bar, watching her staff as they worked. They didn't like it when she was on the floor, but it was good to remind them all she was paying attention. A movement caught the corner of her eye; one of the servers was waving her over. She made her way across the room, turning sideways to slide between tables and pasting a smile on her face. The server who had waved was Janice, another long-time employee. Lucy recognized the couple that she was standing with, the Morton's. They were an older couple who came in every Sunday after church and a stroll along the waterfront. *Damn,* Lucy thought, *I wonder if they go to St. Mark's.*

"Mr. and Mrs. Morton, welcome! How is everything tasting today?" Lucy raised her voice a little, knowing that the husband was a little hard of hearing.

"Everything is excellent, Lucy, dear, as usual. We were wondering, though, where is Donovan? He didn't tell us he was taking time off." Mrs. Morton asked, with a concerned look on her face.

Oh man, Lucy thought. She had expected questions from the customers, but not so soon. It hadn't even been a day. She smiled a little wider and bent down a little bit, so she was closer to eye level with the couple.

"Mrs. Morton, I have some terrible news. I hate to have to tell you this, but Donovan passed away last night. He...he's gone."

Mrs. Morton gasped while Mr. Morton choked on a sip of his wine. "What? What happened? Oh my goodness. Was he ill?" Mr. Morton spoke now, his first words since Lucy had approached. He was always the quieter of the two.

"He wasn't ill. The police don't know exactly what happened yet, but they think it was foul play. He was stabbed." Lucy wasn't sure, exactly, if she should be sharing so many of the details that she had learned from Officer Fitz, but he hadn't told her to keep them quiet. Besides, she had told everything to Ally, so the entire kitchen staff would know all the details by now and every restaurant employee in Boston's North End would know them by morning.

"How horrible. How truly dreadful. I am so sorry for your loss, Lucy. We will miss him. Donovan was always so good to us." Mrs. Morton used her napkin to dab a tear from her eye.

Oh, settle down, Mrs. Morton. You only knew him as a handsome man with a fake Italian accent who gave you too many complimentary glasses of white wine, Lucy thought to herself. Out loud, she spoke, thanking Mrs. Morton for her kind words and moving away from the table as quickly as she could. She returned to her spot behind the bar, knowing that any minute the tourists would arrive and there would be a line out the door.

Chapter 4

Lucy was sitting again, in her office chair, her nightly ritual. She could hear the servers outside, jostling around and shuffling their receipts and sales reports together for her, but they were more subdued than usual. Many of them had looked up to Donovan, with his easy-going ways and steady demeanor. Everyone else had gone home, and so the servers were the only staff left in the restaurant, aside from a few dishwashers who were working on cleaning the floors. The servers had to stay until their last tables left and then flip the restaurant and get it ready for the following night. They would put out the linens and set the tables, put the bottles of white wine in the wine coolers under the server stations, refill the salt and pepper shakers, everything it took to get the restaurant ready to open again. However, this time they did it with a little more energy—tomorrow was Monday, the day the restaurant was closed and so everyone's day off.

Intuitively Lucy stood up and stepped outside the office. "Hey guys?" she called out. The servers all stopped what they were doing and looked at her expectantly. "Hey guys, I just wanted to say thank you for all of your hard work. I know it was a tough night without Donovan. Everyone really stepped up and I really appreciate it. I know we're all going to miss Donovan, and it's going to be hard to move forward without him. He was really one of the few who kept this place going." She paused and swallowed hard, feeling tears start to prick behind her eyes.

"But we have to keep going, and we have to remember Donovan. We have to remember how much he loved this place and carry that love forward with us, and use it to remember him." She tried her best to smile at everyone and waved. "Now go home! We had a great night and tomorrow is Monday…have a great day off, everyone." Lucy went back in to the office and sat down, collecting the server's papers and stacking them up in front of her. The kitchen got quieter as the last of the employees left for the evening. Ally had left earlier, so Lucy was all alone in the office. Once all the servers had left, she reached out and switched on the portable radio that sat on the desk between her computer and Ally's. This was her favorite time of the night, when the rest of the world was asleep and she was all alone to finally get some work done.

Close to two a.m., Lucy leaned back in her chair and closed her eyes. *Finally done.* She'd had an early start this morning, thanks to Officer Fitz, and was exhausted. She considered making another cup of coffee. *No,* she thought, *if I can't remember how many cups I've had today I probably shouldn't have another.* Her eyes still closed, her mind started to wander, remembering her last conversation with Donovan. He had seemed calm, relaxed, certainly not a man involved in something that was about to get him murdered. Lucy's thoughts drifted back over the years she had known Donovan, and how hard they had both worked to get this restaurant on the map, until she fell asleep right there in her desk chair.

Crash! Lucy woke with a start and opened her eyes. What was that noise? She rubbed her eyes and shifted around in the chair, trying to loosen up her stiff back. *Ugh, why do I always fall asleep in this damn chair?* she thought to herself. Lucy listened, but didn't hear anything else. The noise must have been a part of whatever she was dreaming about.

Lucy got up and left the office, locking the door behind her. She walked over towards the back door, pausing as she passed the stairs down to the basement, what was that light down there? Had one of the servers left the basement light on again? They all knew the rule, last one to leave turns out the light. *Oh well*, Lucy thought, *sure, guys, I'll get it, no problem*. She started to head down the stairs, ignoring the loud creaks as the treads protested against her weight. As the noise rang out, all of a sudden the light she could see over near the lockers flickered and shook, almost like it had been moved. At the same time, Lucy noticed something that looked wrong. There was a shadow over near the corner where there shouldn't be anything at all.

Lucy took another step downwards, and the light and the shadow both took off towards the back wall, where there was a window in the upper part that opened out to the street.

"Hey, stop!" Lucy shouted as she ran down the stairs. What she would do if they did stop, she had no idea. "Stop, get back here!" She got to the bottom of the stairs and took off across the room just as the shadow, which was now looking more and more like a person, got to the window. They jumped up and grabbed the sill, pulling themselves through with surprising athleticism for someone so tall. Lucy got to the window just as they stood up outside and took off down the street.

"Goddamn it!" Lucy cursed out loud to an empty room. What had they been after? The lockers were down here, but so was all the wine for the restaurant - some bottles worth thousands of dollars. Lucy turned around and surveyed the room, looking for anything out of place. The door to the wine cellar looked just fine, still locked like she had left it after dinner service.

The lockers, however, were another story. Half of them hung open, and Donovan's locker was missing its door altogether. A pair of bolt cutters lay abandoned on the floor where the intruder must have dropped them. Maybe that had been the noise that awakened Lucy. The floor under the window shimmered with shattered glass.

Shit, she thought. *What did they get?* She surveyed the lockers. Most of them still seemed full, or at least, they still had plenty of things in them. She touched the corner of Donovan's nearly empty locker. *I should pack up his things and take them upstairs.*

Lucy looked again at the nearly empty locker. *Wait a second.* The only thing in Donovan's locker was the pair of dress shoes she had noticed that morning. The hat, the one with the eye-catching logo and bright colors, was missing. *Weird,* Lucy thought. Who on earth would steal a ratty old baseball cap, but leave the nice-looking shoes?

Suddenly, a thought popped into Lucy's head. *Damn. The cops are going to come back. Twice in one day. What are the neighbors going to think?*

Chapter 5

"Hello again, ma'a...I mean, Lucy." Officer Fitz smiled as he greeted Lucy. This time, he wasn't alone. He was accompanied by another officer in a uniform, and a man in a suit. "Lucy, these are my colleagues, Officer Simmons and Detective Carter. Detective Carter is handling Donovan's case. Since these two incidents seem related, he'll be investigating the break-in as well. Officer Simmons is here to assist, and I came along to make all the introductions."

Officer Simmons was tall and lanky, with blonde hair. He was pale, with a long face and a sharp nose. His ill-fitting uniform was tucked into his pants and cinched tight with a dark belt.

Detective Carter was the total opposite of the officer he stood next to. He was short and round, with dark hair and a red face. He tugged at the red and blue striped tie around his neck, loosening it as he read the notebook in his other hand. Lucy recognized it as the notebook that Officer Fitz had been taking notes in this morning.

"Ms. Moretti, Officer Fitz here has briefed me on the conversation you had this morning. I'm very sorry for your loss." Detective Carter paused and sniffled before continuing. "Can you tell me what you saw this evening during the break-in?" He handed Officer Fitz's notebook back as he spoke,

Lucy took a deep breath. "Well, detective, it was right around two, maybe two fifteen this morning. I was sitting here, in my office. To be honest, I was sleeping."

At this, Officer Fitz, standing behind the detective, smiled. "I heard this loud noise from the basement, maybe the window breaking, and I started to go downstairs. Whoever it was heard me coming and ran towards the window. I tried to stop them, I don't know why, and they grabbed the windowsill, and climbed out. I didn't see who it was."

The detective nodded as he took notes in his own notebook. "And did you notice what this person was wearing?" he asked.

"Not really. It was dark, and I believe they were wearing dark clothing. But I only saw them for a minute." Lucy looked up at all three officers as they watched her speak.

"Thank you. Are you able to tell if anything was taken from the lockers, or from the wine cellar downstairs?" the detective asked.

"Only one thing. There was a baseball cap in Donovan's locker...Officer Fitz and I noticed it together this morning. As for all the lockers, I don't know exactly what was in them. I'll have to ask all my employees when they come in on Tuesday. We're closed tomorrow, on Mondays, so everyone has the day off."

"The hat's not important. Just let me know once you've spoken to your employees about anything else that may be missing. We'll take some photographs and some fingerprints from downstairs and then we'll be out of your hair. Thank you very much for your assistance." The detective closed his notebook and stuffed it into one of his pockets. All three men filed back down the basement stairs to the scene of the crime, leaving Lucy alone in the office.

Lucy leaned back in her chair and closed her eyes. It was getting close to five in the morning, and she had been up since Officer Fitz had pounded on her door before ten o'clock that morning. At least she had taken a nap before the break-in.

She could hear the three men down in the basement, taking measurements, and bickering over who was going to take the fingerprints. It sounded like they had been working together for a long time.

"Damn it, Simmons! Just take the prints so we can go home!" The detective's voice echoed up the stairs as he raised it in frustration. "Some of us have wives to go home to, unlike you two putzes."

"Can it, Carter. *Some* of us are doing just fine for ourselves, thank you very much," Officer Simmons' voice responded. Officer Fitz seemed to be staying out of it.

"Anyway, I'm just about done. Start packing up, we'll be done at the same time." Officer Simmons sounded satisfied with himself.

A few minutes later, the three men trooped back up the stairs. "Ms. Moretti, we'll be getting out of your hair now. I know you've had a long day. Officer Fitz has your contact info, so don't worry about that. I'll be in touch personally with any information or updates. Gentlemen, let's be on our way."

"Thank you all very much for coming out so late. Or early, as it were. Let me lock up and I'll walk out with you." Lucy turned off the light in the basement stairs, and the one in the office. She locked the door behind her and turned to follow the officers to the back door. Detective Carter opened the door and walked through it, letting it swing close behind him, until Officer Simmons caught it, and did the same. Officer Fitz was third, and caught the door, but he held it open, gesturing for Lucy to go through first.

"Thank you, Officer. Much appreciated." She smiled at him as he went through the door.

"Detective, I'll be right behind you. I'll walk Lucy up the stairs and check out her apartment. I don't want to take any risks after the break-in downstairs."

The thought hadn't even occurred to Lucy that someone might have also tried to break in upstairs. Maybe after she'd chased them off downstairs, they had come up here to try again.

Officer Fitz went up the stairs first, one hand resting on the butt of his gun in its holster. *He's really taking this seriously,* Lucy thought.

He reached the door at the top and tried to turn the handle. Nothing happened; it was still locked.

"Looks like no one got in this way. Are there any other points of entry?" He turned to face her.

"Nope," she said, "Just the windows facing the street, and no one could have gotten to those."

"Do you mind if I unlock it and just take a look around?" he asked, holding out his hand for the keys.

"Of course," Lucy answered. She dropped the keys into his outstretched hand and watched as he tried to unlock the door.

"Here, it sticks," she said, "Let me get it."

"No, no, I've got it!" he answered as the lock finally turned in the door. He glanced at her with a triumphant grin and pushed the door open. He turned back to the apartment, his hand going back to the butt of his gun as he took a step inside. He reached next to the door, feeling for a light switch. He found it, flooding the room with light. Officer Fitz took a look around and stepped into the apartment. He checked the two tiny bedrooms and the bathroom, trying the windows as he reached them. Finally he returned to the doorway where Lucy waited.

"Alright, I'm satisfied. You should be safe here. Just make sure you lock the door behind me, and leave all the windows locked as well." He smiled at her again.

"Thank you so much for everything, Officer Fitz. I really do appreciate all the help," Lucy said, smiling back as his grin widened.

"My pleasure, ma'am. Have a good night. Don't be afraid to reach out if you need anything." He shook her hand, leaving a business card behind in hers. "That's my direct number." He took off down the stairs, taking them two at a time.

"Very smooth, Officer Fitz!" Lucy called after him, smiling a real smile for the first time all day. She went back inside the apartment as the three officers pulled away, making sure to lock the door behind her.

Chapter 6

Lucy lay in bed, refusing to open her eyes and check the time. She was exactly where she had fallen asleep, with the pillow pulled over her head to block out the morning light she knew would be peeking through the windows. One of these days she would get around to putting up blinds to replace the curtains her grandmother had sewn for the windows. Not today, though.

She rolled over, tucking the pillow below her head. The analog alarm clock on her night table read just past eleven o'clock in the morning. Along with the curtains, it was another remnant of her grandparent's time in this apartment.

Only eleven, Lucy thought. *Still a few more hours until Ally gets here.* Lucy and Ally always spent their days off together in the apartment. Ally would test new recipes, and Lucy would work on everything else that was required to keep the place running, ordering all the various odds and ends they needed or working through the numbers for the restaurant. Since Ally left work earlier at night and Lucy stayed to shut down the restaurant, Ally would do the early morning trip to the farmer's market downtown and Lucy would sleep in. They would meet after lunch at the apartment and work together until it was time to enjoy the meal for dinner. Sometimes the recipe would make it onto the menu, and sometimes the recipe would go straight in the trash. It was always a toss-up until they sat down to eat.

But in the meantime, Lucy headed straight for the bathroom. She took a long, hot shower, letting the water wash over her until she finally started to feel a little better. She kept replaying in her head everything that had happened the day before, starting and ending with that Officer Fitz. *I think I spent more time with him than I did with anyone else yesterday*, she thought to herself. He had been helpful, coming back with the detective the second time after the robbery.

Lucy got out of the shower and wrapped herself up in her bathrobe before heading out to the kitchen and starting the coffee maker. Downstairs in the restaurant, coffee was carefully ground and brewed using imported Italian beans, but up here in her apartment, it was regular store brand, pre-ground coffee. She almost preferred what she kept in the apartment, and either way, it was cheaper.

She watched the coffee drip down into the pot, waiting impatiently. She poured it out into a mug and headed to the couch. She sank down into the cushions and switched on the TV, flipping through the channels as she blew on her coffee. All of a sudden, Donovan's face filled the screen - she had landed on the local news. Lucy stayed on the channel, listening while the anchor went on and on about Donovan without really saying anything. The anchor said more about Alba than she did about Donovan himself. *Oh, well, a little publicity never hurts.*

The more she thought about it, absentmindedly sipping her coffee, the more Lucy realized that she didn't really know much about Donovan at all. For having known him since she was a teenager, Lucy couldn't think of a single fact about him that the news anchor hadn't just repeated on the air. Born in Vermont, lived in Boston since he was a teenager. Started at Alba at nineteen and had worked there ever since. The news had even interviewed one of their customers outside the restaurant.

Lucy and Donovan had always talked, had even had long conversations late into the night after the other servers had left, but Lucy still knew almost nothing about Donovan. He had been such a private person; an expert at carrying on life without passing on any information about himself.

And what about that hat she had found in his locker yesterday? The one that went missing after the robbery last night. It looked like it belonged to a baseball league or something. How had he never mentioned that? Did he play on a team down in Redmond?

Lucy's mind continued to wander as she sat on the couch, thinking over Donovan's life and the little she knew about it. She knew he had been single, but Lucy hoped he had had a friend who he confided in, someone he had really been able to talk to. She was lucky enough to have that person in Ally for years, and she couldn't imagine having to handle this situation without someone to talk it over with.

There was a knock on the door, interrupting her thoughts. Lucy glanced at the clock, almost noon. *Who could it be? It's too early for Ally.* She waited for a second to see if the knock would come again. She didn't get people knocking too often, with a door opening on to a balcony over an alley like it did. Yesterday had certainly been an exception, and twice in two days was unheard of.

Instead of another knock, she heard the sound of a key sliding into the lock and the tumblers turning. The door opened to reveal Ally, loaded down with bags.

"You're up already! I was going to surprise you with breakfast." Ally exclaimed, coming in through the door and dropping the bags on the kitchen counter.

"If I shut my eyes, will it still count?" Lucy asked, smiling.

"No!" Ally exclaimed. "But I'll still make it for you anyway. Your favorite, brown sugar waffles with peaches and cream." The dish was a specialty of Ally's, one she had developed when she was living in Savannah, Georgia after she left Charleston.

"Mmh," Lucy groaned, her mouth watering. "Can I help?" She got up off the couch and started across the small living room to the kitchen.

"No way! Sit back down. You had to spend practically all day with that dreadful cop yesterday and then run a dinner service. Relax," Ally called as she started unpacking the bags.

"You don't even know the half of it, Ally. The cops were here again last night, after everyone left. There was a break-in in the basement."

"Holy crap, Luce! What? What happened?" Ally dropped the bag of peaches she was holding and rushed over to the couch where Lucy was sitting.

"It's fine. Really. Someone, some guy I think, came in through the window and broke open some of the lockers. It doesn't look like he actually took anything, which is weird. All that was missing was a baseball cap from Donovan's locker." Lucy shrugged and stepped across the kitchen, sitting on one of the stools at the tiny island that divided the kitchen and the living room.

"It really wasn't that big of a deal, surprisingly." she continued. " Any other day it would have been huge news. I called the cops and they sent the same officer from yesterday morning, a guy, Fitz, and another officer and a detective. It's the same detective from Donovan's case since they thought it might be related. They told me they'll let me know if they turn anything up."

"Lucy, you can't catch a break!" Ally poured herself a cup of coffee and leaned against the counter as she sipped. "You're handling all this remarkably well. Two days ago the most exciting thing that had happened all week was when the produce delivery was late."

Lucy smiled. Ally was right.

"Oh well. Life happens. At least it wasn't me who got stabbed to death." They both laughed out loud at that, as morbid as it was. At least they were still laughing after the weekend they had been through.

Chapter 7

"Ally, as always, that was wonderful." The two women were sitting on the couch, since Lucy didn't have a dining room, or a dining room table. The apartment was way too small for that. Their dirty dishes on the coffee table in front of them, both women leaned back against the couch and relaxed.

"What do you say we leave the dishes for later?" Lucy asked. "I could really use some sunshine. It feels like it's been days since I was outside in the sunlight. Want to take a walk?" she asked.

"Definitely. We can work off some of these waffles too. And all that whipped cream—ugh! " Ally got up off the couch and stacked the dirty plates together, heading to the kitchen.

"Slow down,how do you have so much energy?!" she called after Ally. More slowly, Lucy pulled herself up off the couch and followed her friend into the kitchen. Ally quickly stacked the dishes up in the sink and rinsed her hands off. "Alright, let's go!"

They both slipped on their shoes and jackets. Boston could get pretty chilly in early summer, especially by the water where they were. They stepped out the door, Lucy pausing to lock it with Officer Fitz's words from the night before echoing in her mind.

Ally headed down the stairs first, Lucy following close behind. Lucy gestured at the back door of Alba as they walked by. "It sure does feel good to be walking right past that door," she commented.

"Doesn't it? Don't even think about the restaurant today," Ally said. "Just think about what a beautiful day it is and how nice it is to be outside."

They reached the end of the alley, both subconsciously turned to the left onto Salem Street, towards the waterfront and away from St. Mark's, where Donovan's body had been found. They strolled along the sidewalk, window shopping and stopping to read the menus of the competing restaurants along the road. The street was home to many of the Italian restaurants located in the North End, including Alba. It ended in an intersection near Charter Street, near the old North Church where Paul Revere's famous signals had hung in 1775.

Even though many of the restaurants in the neighborhood hadn't had a menu change since the eighties, Lucy and Ally still liked to keep up on the competition. It was impossible to tell when a decades-old restaurant might be sold, or taken up by an over-zealous grandchild who wanted to prove they could handle the family business.. Lucy was lucky. So far, the small changes she had been making to the restaurant, things like new specials, cutting back on the expensive ingredients, cutting back on the hours her staff worked, were working without any fallout. She had finally taken over a little less than three years ago, and was working to improve the restaurant where she could.

The two women strolled along the street, making a few more turns, to the small park where the North End met the Boston Harbor. They laughed as they walked, gossiping about whether or not one of the new busboys would work up the courage to ask out the red-headed bartender he was so obviously had a crush on.

"No way, he'll never do it! He's afraid to ask her for a glass of water," Ally scoffed.

"I don't know, Al, last week they were talking an awful lot. I think she might return the feelings…who knows what could be blossoming behind the bar!" Both women laughed.

"Man, like we have any room to talk. When was the last time you went on a date, huh? College?" Ally teased.

"I had coffee with Lucas from next door just two weeks ago, and you know it! I just haven't had a chance to call him back," Lucy defended herself. Lucas was the manager of the restaurant next to Alba.

"Please! You know very well that was not a date. He wanted your permission to put the dumpster for their renovation outside the back door!" Ally laughed as she spoke.

"Yeah, and I told him I'd get back to him and let him know! He hasn't had a chance to ask me out again, because I haven't called," Lucy laughed, trying to explain herself, but Ally wouldn't let her off the hook. She didn't have any real interest in Lucas, but he was a convenient excuse to keep Ally from getting on her case about dating.

"Oh please, we're both married to the job. I haven't been on a date in years. I've stayed up all night with plenty of men though—at least in the kitchen!" Ally joked.

They laughed together and watched the boats moving across the harbor.

Lucy spotted something familiar, out of the corner of her eye. Blue and purple, moving quickly through the crowd of tourists at the water's edge. Even this early in the season it was hard to navigate around them.

Wait a second, Lucy thought, *that's the hat.* It was a blue and purple baseball cap, with the same logo that had been on the cap stolen from Donovan's locker. It was being worn by a teenage boy, who couldn't have been older than sixteen. Lucy started towards him to ask about the cap, was it from a team or something? Had the boy known Donovan?

The boy was tall, with long legs that allowed him to move quickly through the crowd. Lucy sped up, Ally trailing behind her. "Luce? Where are we going?"

"That hat! It's the same one I told you about, from Donovan's locker. I think that boy might have known him!" Lucy called back over her shoulder.

The boy turned at the mention of Donovan's name, he had been close enough to hear. When he saw Lucy coming towards him, he ripped the hat off of his head and shoved it into his pocket, starting to run back towards the crowded city streets surrounding the park.

"Wait! I want to talk to you!" Lucy shouted desperately, hoping he would come back. Instead the mysterious boy just picked up speed, dodging through the crowd with impressive dexterity. He jumped out into the street just as a tour bus came by, running past it and disappearing into the city on the other side.

"Damn!" Lucy cried as she slowed to a halt, slowly noticing she was being watched by all the tourists.
Ally caught up with her. "Lucy? What was that all about? I know it's been a while since you had a date, but you don't need to chase them through the crowds! Besides, don't you think he was a little young for you?" Ally joked, wheezing as she caught her breath.

Lucy reached out and playfully punched her friend in the arm. "Shut up! That wasn't why I was chasing him, obviously. It was his hat—that was the same hat I told you about, that I saw in Donovan's locker. I'm pretty sure it was the only thing that was actually stolen during the break-in. I thought maybe it was a team or something, maybe they played like softball or something. I just wanted to ask him if he knew Donovan." Tears pricked at Lucy's eyes as she spoke. She hadn't realized how upset she was about the murder.

"I mean, what if he still has family, or friends," she continued, "that he never told us about but are expecting him to come by, or to call, or to show up for softball practice. It just breaks my heart that it seems like he had no one."

"I know, Luce. I know. It's horrible. But we've done all we can, for the time being. The police are working on it and I'm sure they'll find out who they should contact. Donovan must have had someone." Ally put her arm around her friend and slowly guided her back on to the sidewalk, back towards the restaurant and Lucy's apartment.

"Let's head back, okay? I still have everything for the special we have to test, the seafood cioppino. It's all in the fridge back at your place. Lucky you—two meals today!" Ally joked, trying to cheer up Lucy, who managed a smile as she wiped away a few stray tears.

"Sure thing, Al. Thanks." Arms still around each other, the two headed back to the cozy, messy apartment above Alba, where they spent the afternoon drinking wine and cooking together.

Chapter 8

Later that night, after Ally had headed back to her own apartment a few blocks away, Lucy sat on the couch, still nursing the last glass of white wine Ally had poured. They had devoured the seafood cioppino Ally had prepared, declaring it a total success. It would be on the menu next week as the dinner special. Ally had called her seafood vendor right then and there from the apartment, sweet talking him into giving her everything she would need on short notice. Lucy was learning a lot about her best friend, like just how many talents she had under that chef's hat.

Lucy was still thinking about that tall, nervous boy in the park. She swore it was the same cap that had been in Donovan's locker, although Ally had gently tried to ask if she could have been mistaken. *No way*, she thought to herself. *I know what I saw, and I know it was the same stupid hat.*

Lucy reached under the coffee table and grabbed her laptop from where it was haphazardly leaning against one of the legs. She booted it up and waited. The thing was ancient and took forever to turn on. It was the same laptop her father had bought for her when she started college.

A picture of the desert finally filled her screen, indicating the computer was ready. Lucy navigated to the search bar on the home screen and typed in 'Redmond, MA recreational baseball,' remembering what the back of the cap had said. The computer loaded the results, and—nothing . A few hits about the local high school baseball team, but that was it. The high school team had a completely different logo, so that definitely wasn't it. Lucy repeated the search again, this time looking for softball instead of baseball. Still, nothing.

Lucy kept trying, long after she finished her glass of wine, trying different search words and different combinations of search words. She had nothing. There was nothing in Redmond that was anywhere close. No little league teams, the high school team with a completely different logo, and no adult recreational leagues. She even tried it without adding the 'MA' to the end, in case somehow Donovan had been involved with a team in a different Redmond in another state. There was absolutely nothing.

I wonder if I could find anything if I went down there, Lucy thought to herself. Impulsively, she picked up her cell phone and dialed Ally's number, tapping her foot while it rang.

"What is it?" Ally's groggy voice filled her ear. "I was sleeping. Is everything okay?"

"Everything is fine...I'm sorry I woke you up. Hey, what do you think about a quick road trip tomorrow morning? We'll be back before noon, I promise," Lucy spoke quickly, tripping over her own tongue in her excitement.

"What? Where to?" Ally asked, her voice a little clearer.

"I was thinking of driving down to Redmond, where Donovan's baseball cap was from. I tried looking it up, but there doesn't seem to be a baseball team or anything the hat might relate to," Lucy explained.

"Luce, you need to let the hat go," Ally said firmly. "It's just a hat, it doesn't have anything to do with the murder."

"I know, I know," Lucy sighed. "But I was thinking, maybe if we could find the team, we could find someone who knew his family. I really want them to know what happened."

"Okay, okay, we can go," Ally sighed. "But I'm not leaving before eight! Come pick me up?"

"You got it. Thank you, Ally. Now go back to sleep!" Ally's muffled curse in response was cut off when Lucy hung up the phone.

Chapter 9

Lucy woke up the next morning feeling excited. *What if Ally and I are actually able to do something helpful?* she wondered to herself as she showered.

Coffee in hand, Lucy descended the back staircase and crossed the alley to where her tiny Camry was parked. Similar to her laptop, it was the car she had owned when she started college.

Still starts, Lucy thought as she turned the key. It was always a minor victory when the car started on the first try. She put it in gear and drove carefully to the end of the alley, where she navigated out onto Salem Street. Ally lived only a few blocks away, and typically Lucy would never drive. It was usually faster to walk anyway, with city traffic the way it was. But today they were venturing outside of their usual stomping grounds, and the car was a necessity to get outside of the city, and down to the South Shore.

A few minutes later, Lucy pulled up outside of Ally's apartment, on nearby Beacon Hill. Ally had scored a teeny, tiny apartment, on the top floor of an equally teeny, tiny apartment building. However, the view was spectacular, and that was all Ally had cared about when she signed the lease.

Lucy shot Ally a quick text. *Outside*, it read. A few minutes later, a breathless Ally popped out of the front door, carrying her own travel cup of coffee.

"Great minds think alike!" Lucy joked when Ally opened the passenger side door, lifting her own cup of coffee.

"Please, like I was leaving the house without it this morning!" Ally called back as she climbed in the car. "When are you getting rid of this hunk of junk anyway? It's practically as old as you are."

"Hey! Never you mind how old this car is, it works perfectly well. Just be grateful we're not taking the train!" The two women grimaced together at the thought of trying to make the trek on Boston's public rail system.

They chatted as Lucy navigated through the twisty Boston streets, making her way to the interstate that led south. As they left the city, high-rises gave way to crowded houses visible from the highway. They traveled for almost an hour, eventually ending up in the coastal city of Redmond, the town that had been on Donovan's hat.

"Well, here we are, Luce. What now?" Ally asked, before finishing the rest of her now-lukewarm coffee while Lucy parked the car.

"Honestly...I'm not exactly sure," Lucy answered uncertainly. "Let's start by finding a diner or something and grabbing some breakfast. We can't investigate on empty stomachs!"

"Investigate? Please!" Ally scoffed. "Soon you'll be on the police force with all your new friends."

"They're hardly my friends, Ally! I can't help it if I've spent more time with them than I have with you these last few days," Lucy laughed as she answered. "Come on, let's go."

Lucy opened her car door and stepped out onto the side street she had parked on. Ally followed suit and they walked together down the street, back towards the center of town.

"Do you see anything promising?" Lucy asked, peering into store fronts as they passed. Most were dark, since it was still morning.

"Up ahead...I think that's a café," Ally said. "Let's go check it out."

They stepped inside and relaxed in the warmth, shaking off the morning chill still in the air.

"Welcome to the Early Bird Cafe!" called out a woman standing behind the counter. She was short, and on the older side, probably in her seventies. She had grey hair and was wearing what seemed to be a hand-knit sweater.

"Please, sit yourselves down anywhere you like. Menus are on the table and I'll be right over with coffee," the woman called out.

Ally and Lucy smiled at her and selected a table in the back corner, where the cold air from the door wouldn't disturb them. The woman came over with a pot of coffee and filled the mugs on the table.

74

"My name is Edith, girls, and I'll be taking care of you today. Take a look at the menu and just give me a shout when you're ready to place your order. Oh, now, let me refill that creamer for you. Pass it over, would you, dear?" Edith asked, gesturing at Ally.

"Oh, of course!" Ally responded, passing it over. Edith grabbed it and bustled away, humming to herself.

"Man, I sure hope we have that much energy when we're old," Lucy said under her breath once the woman was out of earshot. "That is truly impressive."

"And kind of scary," Ally agreed, picking up her menu. "What are you thinking?" she asked.

Lucy glanced down at the menu she had absentmindedly picked up. "I think an omelet might be good. Maybe with bacon and Swiss? Ooh, and onions and peppers, too," she said. "How about you?"

"Pancakes," Ally said decisively. "This is the kind of place that always has great pancakes."

"Edith?" Lucy called out. The older woman's head popped out from around the door into the kitchen.

"All set, dear?" she asked, hurrying across the small restaurant. "What can I get for you?"

"I'll have an omelet, with bacon, Swiss, peppers, and onions. Rye toast, please," Lucy responded, holding out the menu for Edith.

"Perfect. And for you, sweetheart?" Edith asked Ally, not bothering to write anything down.

"Pancakes for me, please!" Ally responded in a chipper voice.

"Got that, hon?" Edith called out suddenly, raising her voice.

"Got it, Edith!" called back a man's voice from the kitchen.

"My husband, Rob," Edith said with a smile. "He cooks, I serve!" she added, before heading back into the kitchen.

"Well, now, isn't that sweet!" Ally said. "Almost reminds me of us," she commented, laughing at Lucy's outraged face.

"Yeah, you would be the husband in this relationship!" Lucy retorted. They both laughed together and leaned back to wait for their food. Edith came back out of the kitchen and stationed herself behind the counter, rolling silverware into napkins.

"So, what brings you girls in today?" she called out. "Usually we don't get too busy on Tuesday mornings," she said, gesturing at the empty restaurant.

"We're actually here to do a little research," Lucy responded before Ally could say anything. "Do you know anything about a town baseball team? A...friend of mine used to play on it, and I'd like to get in touch with him again," Lucy improvised, feeling bad for telling a white lie to such a sweet old lady.

"Well, now, you came to just the right place," Edith responded. She called back into the kitchen, "Rob! Get out here! These ladies want to ask you a question."

Lucy shot Ally a questioning look. Why did Edith think that Rob would have the answers? Ally responded by raising her eyebrows and shrugging. "Hey, you're the one who wanted to come down here," Ally whispered across the table.

An older man came out of the kitchen, wearing a plaid shirt and a white apron. "Why hello there, ladies," he said, in an accent that was straight out of the deep South. "What can I do for you today?"

"We're here looking into a town baseball team," Lucy said. "A friend of mine used to play on it."

"Well then, you certainly have come to the right place. I coached the rec baseball team, for as long as we had one," Rob said, leaning against the counter.

"Had to shut the team down about five, six years ago," he continued. "Town didn't want to pay for it anymore."

"What a shame," Ally said, turning to face Rob and Edith. "My dad used to play for a similar league back in my hometown, and he loved it."

"Yep, sure were a lot of good memories with that team," Rob replied. "But anyway, who are you tryin' to get in touch with? I still have contact info for a lot of those guys."

"Did anyone named Donovan Fagan ever play with you?" Lucy asked hopefully.

"Well now, that name doesn't ring a bell." Rob moved across the small dining room, near the table that Ally and Lucy sat at. He walked past them and took something down off the wall, passing it over to Lucy.

"That's the last team picture we took, a few years ago. Most of those guys had been on the team for a decade, at least," Rob said.

Lucy grabbed the picture eagerly, positioning it between herself and Ally so they could both look. Suddenly, something in the photograph caught Ally's eye. Every team member was wearing a matching baseball cap, but they looked nothing like the one she had found in Donovan's locker. These caps were red, with a black brim, and the words "Redmond Baseball" written across the front in black text.

"I don't see him," she said, pointing the picture more towards Ally. "Do you recognize anyone?"

"Nope, Donovan definitely isn't in this picture," Ally replied.

"What interesting caps," Lucy commented. "Who designed them?"

"Why, I did, with Edith's help, of course," Rob replied, smiling at his wife. "We designed them the very first year we played, and kept the same hats through to the end. I still have a box of 'em at home."

"Wonderful," Lucy said, feeling her spirits fade. There was no way Donovan had been on this team, or that his hat had come from them.

"Too bad you don't see your friend," Rob commented, picking the picture up and returning it to its spot on the wall. "I can ask around and see if anyone else remembers him."

"Thanks, Rob," Ally said, noticing Lucy's disappointment. "We really appreciate it."

"My pleasure, girls. Now let me get back to your breakfast!" Rob replied, heading back into the kitchen.

"You girls need a refill?" Edith called out.

"No thanks, Edith, I think we're all set for right now," Lucy called back.

"Of course. I'll be right out with the food," Edith replied, disappearing back into the kitchen.

Ally and Lucy sat in the quiet restaurant, both looking down at their cups of coffee.

"Well, that was a total bust," Ally said.

"We didn't learn anything. We still don't know where he got the hat, and it looks like it's not even a design the team ever used," Lucy replied, thinking.

"Does that mean he designed his own hat, with a fake logo?" she wondered out loud. "How bizarre."

"There was a lot more to Donovan than we ever knew," Ally replied thoughtfully. Lucy sipped from her coffee mug.

"That's for sure.".

Chapter 10

After finishing their breakfast, which turned out to be delicious, Lucy and Ally hopped back into the car and made the return trip into the city. Soon enough, Lucy found herself standing by the host stand and greeting the first guests of the dinner crowd. At the back of the line, she spotted a familiar face in a blue uniform, Officer Fitz. She gestured at him to come inside and skip the line.

"Thanks for rescuing me," he said, smiling as he spoke. "I thought I would have to wait out there for a while!"

"My pleasure. What brings you back to Alba? Looking for a good meal? I promise we have the best!" Lucy couldn't help but smile at his infectious grin. "No, no, I'm not here to for any food. I mean, I'm sure it's delicious, but ..."he trailed off, still smiling, but a little more bashfully this time.

"Of course not. Sorry, it's instinct at this point to try and sell a meal. What can I help you with?" She stepped back into the restaurant, away from the doorway as another group tried to enter. Officer Fitz stayed where he was, blocking their way, until she gently touched his arm and pulled him towards her. He looked confused for a second, until the group made their way around him and stepped inside.

"Oh, excuse me," he said to the group as he moved aside, both of them standing next to the end of the bar now. To Lucy, he said "I found myself down the street and just wanted to swing by and check in. Has anything else suspicious happen since the break-in, the night of the murder?"

Another couple standing nearby looked up sharply at the word 'murder'.

"Here, come with me. Back to my office. It's a little quieter there," Lucy said, looking pointedly at the guests around them.

"Oh, of course. My bad. No one wants to talk about murder over dinner. Trust me, I know all too well!" the officer joked. They walked together back through the seating area, pausing as Lucy greeted guests. They made their way through the kitchen, where Ally, working on the line with one of the younger cooks, caught Lucy's eye. She furrowed her brow at the sight of the police officer. Lucy shrugged and gestured to her friend to keep working. Lucy would fill her in after the officer left.

They both sat down inside the office, Lucy at her desk and Officer Fitz at Ally's.

"Sorry about that," he said, gesturing out at the restaurant.

"No problem," Lucy replied. "Thank you for coming by. I appreciate it. We haven't had any problems here at the restaurant. Everything has been running smoothly. Of course, we were closed yesterday, so things couldn't have gone too poorly!" Lucy smiled and chuckled a little at her joke, and the officer responded with a chuckle of his own.

"Good, I'm glad. You said no problems here, though. Does that mean there have been problems outside the restaurant?" he asked.

"No, nothing really. It's just that yesterday, I thought I saw a kid wearing the same hat that went missing from Donovan's locker. The one you and I saw in the morning that day, and that was gone when you were back in the evening. I tried to talk to him, to see if maybe he knew Donovan, but he ran away—literally ran—as soon as I tried to talk to him. It was nothing, just a little weird." Officer Fitz watched her intently as she spoke, his face suddenly serious.

"No, that's not nothing. You're right, it's strange. Where did you see the boy?" he asked, pulling out the small notebook that he seemed to perpetually keep in his left pocket.

"Down by the water, in the part at the end of Hull Street. He ran back into the city, away from the water. He was running so fast he almost got hit by one of those tour busses."

Officer Fitz nodded as he jotted down notes.

"Very interesting. I think that might be important. If I gave you my phone number, would you be willing to keep an eye out for this boy again, and call me if you see him?" he asked.

"Of course. I appreciate you taking this seriously. I know Detective Carter didn't seem to think it was very important," she said.

"Detective Carter sometimes spends too much time looking at the big picture, and not enough time looking for details," Officer Fitz said, clearly trying to be professional when speaking about his boss. Lucy noticed a little smile pulling at the corner of his mouth while he spoke.

Officer Fitz continued, "I know I gave you my business card the other day, but the only phone number on that is for the precinct. I'll give you my cell number—call anytime. I live in the area so even if I'm off duty I can swing by."

"Oh no, I'm sure that won't be necessary. But thank you." Lucy took the piece of paper he offered, with his cell phone number jotted under his name, and slipped it into her pocket.

"My pleasure. Has anything else strange happened?" he asked as he stood up.

"No, nothing at all. Thank you very much for coming by, I really appreciate it," Lucy said as they left the office. Several of the cooks watched curiously; police officers were pretty unusual in the kitchen at Alba.

"Would you mind if I go out the back door? Seems a little quieter. And besides, you don't need people seeing cops come in and out of your restaurant. No offense, but it's not really a great look," Officer Fitz said, smiling again.

"Of course not. It's right over there—well, you know where it is. Just be careful walking, the floor is probably slippery. Thank you again for coming out. I'll be sure to call you if anything strange happens, or if I see that kid again."

"Hey, protect and serve, that's what we're here for. Have a good night, now." Officer Fitz waved as he left through the back door.

Lucy meandered over to where Ally stood waiting for her, having finished her unique critique of the new cook—part dressing down, knocking back his overconfidence a bit, and part encouragement, show him that he still has potential. Her ability to teach cooks like that was one of the many reasons Lucy had asked Ally to join her in Boston.

"Well? What did he want? Did someone else get murdered?" Ally asked expectantly.

"No, Ally, no one else got murdered, no one else got murdered," Lucy responded, rolling her eyes. "He just came by to see if anything else had happened. Said he was in the neighborhood."

"In the neighborhood? That's a flimsy excuse if I've ever heard one. I think he has a crush on you. He's kind of cute, in his own way," Ally teased.

"Oh, shut up! He's just being nice. Besides, something did happen. That weird kid in the park, remember?" Lucy prodded her friend.

"Luce, that was nothing. He ran away because a crazy lady in the park yelled at him. You would have run away, too." Ally replied.

"Whatever! He gave me his phone number to call if something else happens. Besides," Lucy paused, "Look over there. Is that supposed to be on fire?" she said, pointing across the kitchen to where a rag sat on the stainless steel counter next to the gas range, merrily burning.

"Shit!" Ally cried as she took off across the kitchen. "Alberto! Where is Alberto? Get over here! You can't light things on fire!"

Lucy smiled as she headed back out to the dining room. Ally had things under control in the kitchen.

The rest of the dinner service passed quickly and uneventfully. A few ruffled feathers with customers, which Lucy smoothed over with kind words and comped dinners. One customer, who fussed over her order, insisted that the server note her allergy to plums, which they didn't even carry in the restaurant, and another who was desperately upset that he couldn't order French toast, for dinner, in an Italian restaurant.

Oh well, Lucy thought to herself after leaving the table with the omelet man. *Can't please them all.* She had offered him the pasta carbonara, which at least had eggs and cheese and meat in it, all the same ingredients, if presented totally differently. But he had pivoted completely, ordering the bucatini topped with shrimp, scallops, and mussels.

After sending all the servers home, Lucy headed upstairs, leaving work at her 'regular' time for the first time in days. Of course, being the owner who lived above the restaurant, no less, she was never truly done working. But,after the last few days, Lucy was just exhausted. There would always be more work, but for tonight all she wanted was a hot shower and to spend some time alone in the apartment, maybe clean up a little. She certainly knew the apartment could use some love.

Locking the door behind her, Lucy sighed and leaned against it, kicking off her non-slip clogs and pulling off the sweater she was wearing over her blouse. She left both next to the door and headed straight to the shower. It always made her feel better to rinse away the heat and smells of the kitchen. No matter how good she knew the food tasted, it always lost some of its charm once all that was left was the smell on her clothes.

After she stepped out of the shower and slipped into her pajamas, Lucy surveyed the apartment. Saying it could use a little love was definitely an understatement. More like it needed a bulldozer.

Man, did it look like this when Officer Fitz was here? Lucy wondered to herself as she started to straighten up. Some dirty dishes to the kitchen, dirty clothes to the hamper, and the contents of the hamper to the washing machine Lucy was lucky enough to have in the apartment. It was rare in the North End, but her father had been sure to install one when he still lived there.

Lucy checked the clock. It was getting close to two in the morning. *Probably time for bed*, Lucy thought to herself. *Just a little more cleaning. I'll go to bed when the washing machine finishes.*

She kept straightening up, wiping down the dust and food crumbs in the kitchen. For a spot that only got used once a week by Ally, the kitchen sure did manage to get messy. Lucy ate almost all of her meals down in the restaurant.

Lucy moved on to the bedroom, where more dirty clothes piled up in the corners and the bed hadn't been made in weeks. She straightened out the sheets and grabbed the dirty glasses littering the night table. She only brought a glass of water to bed about once a week, so who knew the last time she had cleaned them up.

The washer dinged, letting Lucy know it was done. While she had a washing machine, there was no matching dryer. There were two hooks in the living room, one on either side, installed by her grandfather before Lucy was even born. A clothesline strung between them. The only reason Lucy remembered to take it down in between loads of laundry was that it went right across the living room, it was impossible to cross the room without running into it.

Lucy quickly put up the clothesline, making sure to leave herself on the right side of it to go to bed. She had made that mistake plenty of times before, forcing herself to either play limbo or take all the clothes back down and undo the line.

She hung the clothes quickly. At this point in her life, having lived in this apartment for most of it, Lucy was pretty sure she qualified as an expert at clothesline hanging. Within ten minutes she was switching off the lights and heading to bed.

Chapter 11

The next morning started off much the same as the previous day, nice and relaxed. Lucy headed down to the restaurant around noon, when the first cooks started coming in. Ally usually got to work bright and early, around nine o'clock, but left earlier than Lucy. Lucy liked to be the last one out at night, and make sure the place was locked up tight.

Lucy walked through the back door and waved at Ally. "Morning, Chef!" she called out.

"Good morning!" Ally called back, without looking up from the pepper she was slicing into delicate strips. "All good last night?" Ally asked.

"Everything was nice and slow. Steady business, happy customers, for the most part. All good. I even got back upstairs early enough to straighten up a little, do some laundry."

"Good for you!" Ally exclaimed, sweeping the sliced peppers up off her cutting board and dropping them into the pot next to her.

"What are you working on?" Lucy asked, "Family meal?"

"You got it," Ally reponsed, picking up the sliced pepper and adding it to a big stainless steel bowl. "Pasta with red pepper sauce, that sauce we did for the special over the weekend. I'll grill some chicken or something to go with it, too."

"Well, hey, it sure smells good!" Lucy commented as she walked past, inhaling the spicy red peppers mixed with garlic and onions.

She headed out to the dining room, which was dark and still this early in the day. None of the employees would be out in the dining room, which was already set for dinner, until they sat down to eat family meal later that afternoon. She headed over behind the bar and set the coffee machine to brew herself a cup. While she waited, she wandered over to the big picture windows out onto Salem Street, watching the early afternoon tourists walk by. This was when the street outside started to get busy, although it was nothing compared to how busy the street would be later that day, around dinner time.

She watched the tourists go by, first a family with young kids, then a couple holding hands and smiling at each other. A few delivery people, bringing packages to and from the various businesses. Then, across the street, a now-familiar sight caught Lucy's eye. A blue and purple baseball cap on the head of a tall, skinny boy who was moving quickly.

"Ally!" Lucy shouted. "Ally, the kid is back!" Lucy ran back to her office, where she had left the slip of paper with Officer Fitz's phone number.

"Ally!" she called again as she dialed.

97

"What? What is it?" Ally reappeared from the walk-in cooler at the end of the kitchen.

"That kid is back," Lucy said as she listened to the phone ring, "The one with the hat. He was outside!" Lucy ran back out to the dining room, still holding her ringing cell phone up to her ear. As she watched the boy disappear down the street, she heard the sound of Officer Fitz's recorded voice start to play.

"You have reached Charlie Fitz. Please leave your name and number and I will return your call as soon as possible."

Charlie, huh, Lucy thought, *I wouldn't have guessed.*

"Officer Fitz," she said into the phone, "This is Lucy Moretti, from Alba. I wanted to let you know that the boy I described to you, with the hat, is outside my restaurant right now, walking down Salem Street towards the Greenway Park. It's around one o'clock right now. I'm going to follow him—please call me back as soon as you get this."

With that, Lucy hung up the phone, calling again to Ally, "Ally, I'm going to go follow him! I left a message for Officer Fitz. I'll be right back!"

Not bothering to wait for a response, or to grab her jacket, Lucy slipped out the front door of Alba. The boy was almost out of sight by now. She walked quickly, trying to catch up with him without getting too close.

Chapter 12

Lucy had never followed someone like this before; it was kind of exciting. *If only I had had time to grab my coffee*, Lucy thought to herself. It was still chilly outside and a nice warm cup of coffee would sure help her keep warm.

She followed the cap, and its wearer, all the way down Salem Street to where it intersected with the Rose Kennedy Greenway, a long skinny park that circled nearly half of the city. After the Big Dig, back in the nineties, took the highway system underground, the leftover space was turned into a park.

The boy turned south along the Greenway, continuing until he reached another section of waterfront, this one where the ferries, whale-watch boats, and the tourist cruises docked.

Where is he going? Lucy wondered. The boy walked straight past the long lines and the tourists, down the ramp to where the small, local commuter ferry to Charlestown was waiting. He walked right on, ignoring the middle-aged man checking tickets.

Lucy waited a second at the top of the ramp, digging through her pocket. She pretended to come up empty-handed, ignoring the fact that there had never been anything in her pockets in the first place, and went over to the ticket booth to buy a ticket. The boy may have snuck on, but it didn't seem like Lucy could get away with the same trick.

Ticket in hand, Lucy boarded the small ferry, sitting as far from the boy as she could. He was slouched over in his seat, baseball cap pulled down low over his eyes. He had his cell phone out and was typing furiously.

Lucy leaned back against her seat, wondering if maybe she shouldn't have boarded a boat with a mysterious teenager she knew nothing about. *Oh well*, *no going back now,* she thought as the boat pulled away from the dock. It navigated slowly away from the wharf, past the much larger boats still being boarded. As it cleared the dock, it picked up speed, bouncing in the various cross-wakes that filled the harbor. The boy pulled his hat down even farther over his face and leaned back. It almost looked like he had fallen asleep.

Ten minutes later, the boat docked north of Boston at Charlestown, near the Navy Yard. Up here the Navy ran a few museums, including two that were on ships. Lucy had been there a long time ago on school field trips, but not since middle school. Remarkably, it still looked exactly the same. Lucy paused for a second while the boy disembarked, taking the opportunity to pull out her phone and shoot a quick text to Officer Fitz. *Took the ferry to Charlestown. Still following the boy.*

The boy got off the boat, turning away from the crowds, up past the various docks and the wharves until he reached the Charlestown Marina. Lucy continued to follow him, wondering if she should be worried he hadn't seemed to notice her, at all. *I guess I'm better at this than I expected,* she thought.

The boy slowed down and turned onto one of the wharves. Lucy paused just past the entrance, unsure of what to do. *Should I follow?*

The boy stopped and turned onto one of the boats, turning towards Lucy in the process. In a panic, she turned to the boat she was standing next to her and climbed aboard, praying that no one else was on the boat. It was a little fishing boat, with a small enclosed cabin and a tiny below deck area for storage. Lucy ducked into the cabin, where she could pretend to be busy while she watched the boy through the windshield. He was on a small speedboat, with nowhere to hide.

Suddenly there was someone else—a man-- on board the boat with the boy. *He must have been sitting down*, Lucy thought. *That's kind of weird. Was he hiding?*

Lucy watched as the boy and the mystery man spoke. They seemed to be arguing, waving their hands around. Lucy fiddled with a map that was lying next to the navigation system in her borrowed boat. *Gosh, I hope the person who owns this boat doesn't show up.*

The man who had been hiding was angry now, jabbing his finger at the boy. His face was turning red as he shouted. Lucy could almost make out the words, the man definitely wanted something from the boy. And she could hear a name, Jordan. *That must be the name of the kid,* Lucy realized. The big man kept taking steps forward, until Jordan was backed up against the edge of the boat and man had a fistful of the boys dark green T-shirt. Finally, the kid seemed to give in, throwing his hands up and shaking his head.

The man took a step back, still gesturing violently at the boy. The boy, Jordan, reached up and took off the purple and blue baseball cap, turning it over so he could reach inside. He was fiddling with something. It almost looked like he was unlatching, or unzipping, or *undoing* something inside the hat. He pulled something out of the hat and held it up to the man, letting him examine whatever it was that was in his hand. Jordan tilted his hand a little, and Lucy spotted something shiny. It was almost glimmering as his fingers held it.

Is that...jewelry? Is that what this whole thing has been about? Lucy wondered.

The big man grabbed whatever it was out of Jordan's hand and shoved it in his pocket. He turned to leave the small speedboat when suddenly, he was staring directly at Lucy. They made eye contact and his face turned an even darker shade of red. He lifted his fist and shook it at Lucy, his rage obvious even across the water between them.

Chapter 13

Screaming, "Go get her!" in a deep voice, trembling with anger, the big man turned and pointed at Jordan. Cramming the hat back on his head, Jordan leapt over the edge of the boat, moving with a sudden urgency that he certainly had not displayed earlier in the day. Lucy rushed out of the cabin and onto the small deck of the boat, but it was too late. Jordan was already on the dock, and she had nowhere to go. Panicking, Lucy spun and faced the water. She paused for a second, weighing her options before making a decision and diving right over the edge of the boat into the cold, choppy water where the Charles River met the Mystic River before both spilled into Boston Harbor. She swam down under the shallow keel of the boat, holding her breath. Lucy came up on the other side of the boat, where it gently bobbed against the dock next to Jordan. She surfaced quickly, hearing both men shouting, and took another deep breath before quickly diving under again, this time swimming under the dock.

She swam along under the dock as quickly and quietly as she could, praying the men would just go away. *Unlikely*, Lucy thought as she moved towards the coast.

Maybe if I can just get to the shore, and somehow climb out and run away before they see me. Really, a terrible plan.

But maybe I can make it work.

She paused under the dock. She was close enough to the shore now that she could almost stand, but that also meant she had nowhere else to run—well, swim, –really—without exposing herself. To see if she could hear the men, Lucy turned her head so one ear was above water.

"Where is that stupid bitch?" asked the deeper voice, the older man who had been shouting.

"I don't know, maybe she got away," replied the younger, more nervous sounding voice.

Must be Jordan, Lucy realized.

She stood as still as she could in the water, balancing on her tip toes. The men walked directly over her, their heavy footsteps causing little pieces of dirt to fall through the cracks in the dock, showering over her face. It was cold in the river water, and Lucy was starting to shiver.

"Wait, Rudy, hold up. There's something down there. I think she's right under us," Jordan's voice rang out over Lucy's head.

'Rudy' is the older guy, Lucy realized, committing his name to memory in case she ever got out of this mess alive.

The footsteps stopped, and there was a loud *CRACK* as something ripped through the boards of the dock next to Lucy. Instinctively she bent her knees, dropping her body below the surface. Lucy pulled herself all the way down to the bottom of the river, praying that bullets couldn't reach her under four feet of water. She only had so much breath, and she was running out. Slowly, so slowly, she rose back up to the surface, tilting her head so only her mouth would rise above the water. As quietly as possible she breathed out and back in before slipping back under the water. She couldn't see the two men above her anymore, on the dock, but that didn't mean they were gone.

Suddenly a new noise filtered through the water. *What is that?* Lucy wondered. Suddenly, she realized. *A siren!*

Lucy tilted her ear above the water, listening. There were a lot of footsteps, but she couldn't quite tell what was happening, hidden under the dock. A voice rang out over her head, one she recognized. "Stop! Don't move or I will shoot!"

Officer Fitz!

Lucy rose up until her entire head was above the water. Footsteps pounded above her again, this time going in the opposite direction, towards the end of the dock. A lot of footsteps, Officer Fitz must have brought some friends.

Lucy could hear the sounds of a scuffle coming from the end of the dock. She strained to hear what was happening…was Officer Fitz winning? How did he even know where to find her?

A loud splash came from the end of the wharf, and Lucy tensed as she saw someone fall from the dock above her down into the water. The person looked big, like it could have been Rudy. But it was quickly followed by another splash, this time a police officer diving into the water far more gracefully. Within seconds the officer had caught up to Rudy, and was handcuffing him under the water.

Impressive.

The officer swam back over to the dock, Rudy in tow. Lucy watched while a set of hands reached down from above and hauled Rudy out of the water and back up on to the dock. The uniformed officer reached up and pulled himself out of the water.

There was a loud thud from the end of the dock, and Officer Fitz called out again. "Lucy? You can come out now. We've got both of them." Lucy felt the corners of her mouth lifting up in a smile.

She slowly swam out from under the dock, hesitant. It certainly sounded like things were under control, but since she was pretty sure she had just been shot at, Lucy thought it might still be a good idea to take things slowly.

"Come on, Lucy. It's okay." Officer Fitz's voice was right above her now. She turned around and saw him there on the dock, crouching down to offer her his hand. "How did you find me?" she asked, still in the water.

"You told me where you were going. And then when I got here, I heard a shot. It was really pretty simple after that," he said, smiling. "Now come on, the water is cold." She reached out and took his hand, letting him help her out of the water as she climbed up.

Down at the end of the dock the two men who had chased her were being loaded into a waiting police car. "Lucy, are these the men who chased you, and fired a weapon at you?" Officer Fitz asked.

"Yes, they are. Check the pockets on the big guy. The kid gave him something while I watched. It sparkled in the sunlight." The officer holding the handcuffs of the larger man, both of them soaking wet, used his free hand to check the man's pockets. He came up with the same sparkle that Lucy had seen, only this time it was a lot closer.

"Diamonds. Cut diamonds. Where did these come from, huh?" The officer asked. The man stayed silent. Jordan stared down at his feet.

"And him," said Lucy, "Check his hat. His name is Jordan. I think the big guy is named Rudy."

The second officer, holding Jordan by his handcuffs, pulled the baseball cap off of his head and tossed it to Officer Fitz. He offered it to Lucy. She took it and flipped it over, searching for the hidden pocket Jordan had used to hide the diamonds. Her fingers felt something strange in the seam and she dug farther, finding the zipper buried under the fabric. Triumphantly she unzipped the seam, opening up a pocket in the side of the hat. She grinned and showed it to the officers.

"This is it, isn't it? You're the one who broke into my restaurant, because you needed the hat back. How was Donovan involved? Why did he have this stupid hat?" Lucy asked Jordan. He kept staring at the ground.

"Answer me!" Lucy started to raise her voice, getting upset. "Tell me how he was involved!" She jabbed the teenaged boy in the chest with the brim of the hat.

"Lucy, step back. He'll tell us what he knows down at the station," Officer Fitz cautioned her, putting his hand on her elbow.

"No, tell me! I deserve answers, and you have them." Lucy looked at Jordan expectantly.

"Don was my cousin. He...I don't know. I don't know who this guy is." Jordan answered nervously.

"Donovan had some deal with him. But he was getting nervous. He left the hat at your restaurant because he thought it would be safe. He told me that if he disappeared, if he had to run away, I needed to get the hat back from Alba. But this guy, he figured out who I was and told me he would kill me too if I didn't give him the hat. That's it. I don't know anything else." Jordan spoke all in a rush, sliding away from the bigger man as he did so.

"You can tell us everything when we get down to the station," said Officer Fitz. He gestured at the two other officers, and they put the handcuffed men into the back of the black and white police car.

The two other officers climbed into the front of the car and drove away, leaving Officer Fitz and Lucy alone at the end of the wharf. "Come on, Lucy, my car is over here. I have a blanket,you need to warm up." He guided her over to a non-descript green sedan and opening up the trunk. "Well, really, it belongs to Detective Carter. I'm not important enough to get a car," he joked, self-deprecatingly.

Officer Fitz pulled a thick, woolen blanket out of the trunk. "Part of every officer's travel kit," he said, unfolding it and wrapping it around Lucy's shoulders.

"Thank you," Lucy said, "for everything, Officer Fitz. Thank you for getting my messages and actually showing up and catching them and everything. Thank you."

"That's what I'm here for. And, Lucy, don't you think it's time you called me by my name? It's Charlie."

"Thank you, Charlie," Lucy said as she looked directly into his eyes and smiled.

Chapter 14

Lucy woke up early the next morning. She had called Ally last night, after everything had happened down at the wharf, explaining briefly, but knew Ally would have so many more questions. After she and Officer Fitz—Charlie—had left the wharf, they had gone down to the police station so Lucy could make a statement. She had had to sit, alone, in an empty office and write down everything that happened to her over the last week. After the first page, Lucy just sat and stared at the notebook, until a few minutes later when Charlie had come in, and sat with her to make her laugh. After that, she felt comfortable enough to write everything down. On her way out of the station, she had seen Jordan and the other man being escorted into the interrogation rooms.

Charlie then took her to a burrito place around the corner from the police station. Lucy demolished her entire burrito and part of his, plus the chips and salsa they ordered. She hadn't eaten anything all day, and was famished.

She had finally gotten home around ten at night, long after dinner service at the restaurant had begun. Skipping the restaurant altogether, Lucy went upstairs to take a long, hot shower and rinse off everything that happened to her. After calling Ally, who at that point had left about ten voicemails on the cell phone that had been destroyed when Lucy dove into the water, Lucy crawled straight into bed and fallen asleep.

And now, it was just after eight in the morning. Lucy was curled up under the blanket on her bed, wishing she could go back to sleep. She could still barely believe that any of it had happened, let alone that she had been chased, and shot at, and had to swim for her life under a dock.

There was a gentle knock on the front door of the apartment. Lucy groaned and pulled the pillow overhead, but there was another knock.

"Lucy?" called a familiar voice, "It's Officer Fitz. Are you up yet?"

Lucy still didn't answer. She was too tired to get up.

"I'm sorry it's so early. I just wanted to make sure you're okay."

At that, Lucy rolled out of bed. She grabbed the bathrobe that was tossed on the end of the bed, wrapping it around herself over her pajamas and walked through the living room to open the door. Officer Fitz stood on the other side, wearing a red T-shirt and jeans. It was the first time Lucy had seen him without his uniform.

"Charlie, good morning. What brings you here?" she asked, yawning.

"I'm sorry it's so early. I just wanted to make sure you were okay after yesterday. An experience like that can hit you really hard the next day. How are you feeling?"

"Come in on. You don't have to stand out there. I'll make some coffee." Lucy stepped away from the door and gestured for Charlie to come inside. "I'm doing alright, I think. Do you know...do we know exactly what happened? Who was that guy, the bigger guy?" The words spilled out as Charlie stepped over the threshold.

She stepped over into the kitchen and switched on the coffee maker. While it burbled softly in the background, Charlie explained just exactly what had happened to Lucy over the past few days.

"So it looks like Donovan was involved in some shady stuff. Obviously. We're still trying to figure out how long he and the bigger man, Rudy, had been involved. But either way, that guy Rudy is bad news. He has a record a mile long. That boat he and Jordan were standing on belongs to him. He uses it to make runs all over the east coast. It seems like he's willing to smuggle anything, as long as there's a customer. This time it was diamonds, from a client here in Boston down to someone in Florida. He was using Donovan to handle the actual pickup, so he wouldn't be connected. It seems like Donovan tried to hold out on him, asked for more money before he would hand over the diamonds."

The coffee machine clicked, indicating it was ready. Lucy reached over and poured the two cups while Charlie continued talking.

"Rudy didn't like it when Donovan tried to get more cash out of him. I'm guessing that Donovan knew that Rudy would try to get to him that night, and panicked. I think he took the steak knife with him when he left Alba, to defend himself. But in the end that turned out to be his downfall. Rudy must have followed him and killed him to try and get the diamonds. But, of course, he had left them in the hat in his locker at Alba.

120

And you heard the rest from Jordan down at the wharf."

Lucy nodded slowly as she sipped her coffee. "Wow," she said out loud, "this week has been *way* more exciting than usual."

Charlie laughed. "Trust me, I'm on the same page. I usually don't have to rescue civilians who follow criminals to drop points for smuggled goods," he said, with a pointed look in Lucy's direction.

"I know, I know. In retrospect, definitely shouldn't have followed the scary looking guy through the city. And onto a boat, too. That was...uh, kind of stupid," Lucy said with a chuckle.

"Yeah, kind of. But it worked out, this time at least." Charlie took a sip of his coffee.

They stood together in silence for a second, sipping their coffee. Lucy pulled her robe tighter, covering the T-shirt she slept in.

"Hey, I'm sorry to have come by so early. It seems like I woke you up," Charlie apologized.

"No, no, no problem. I'm glad that you came by," Lucy said, trailing off.

"There was another reason, too. I wanted to check on you. But I was also wondering, uh, if maybe, uh, you'd like, to maybe, sometime, uh, come out to dinner with me," Charlie said, his voice lower than normal.

"Oh," said Lucy. She took a sip of her coffee. Was Officer Fitz really interested in her? He was certainly nice, and he had saved her life the other day. He had shown up when she needed him. And Ally had said that he had a crush on her...could it be true?

"You, uh, you definitely don't have to. Definitely not," Charlie said.

"No, I want to. Let's do it. Are you free on Monday night? That's my day off." Lucy smiled up at him. "I really want to. As long as we go somewhere besides my restaurant," she said, laughing.

"Of course. We'll go anywhere you want. Anywhere at all," Charlie said quickly, looking relieved. "And yes, Monday night is perfect. Can I pick you up? Would seven o'clock work?

"Yes, seven o'clock is perfect. And the place is up to you, your choice," Lucy said.

"Great," Charlie replied. "I know a place." He tilted his cup up and finished the rest of his coffee. "But now I have to get to work. I'll see you on Monday night. I'm looking forward to it." He smiled at her, putting his empty coffee cup in the sink as he headed towards the door.

Lucy stayed where she was, leaning against the counter. She smiled back at him. "So am I. I'll see you then."

Charlie headed out through the door, carefully closing it behind him.

Lucy smiled to herself and took another sip of her coffee. *I have a date*, she thought. *Wow, that's something new. Ally will be so impressed.*

Lucy finished her coffee, but stayed where she was in the kitchen, a smile on her face. She waited until she was sure Officer Fitz was gone, then headed through the front door, not bothering to change out of her pajamas, or even put on shoes. She got to the bottom of the stairs and opened the back door to the restaurant.

"Ally!" Lucy called, seeing Ally's blonde curls across the kitchen. "Man, do I have a lot to tell you!" Lucy continued, grinning.

A NOTE TO THE READER

I hope you have enjoyed Murder at St. Mark's!
Please consider leaving a review by following the link
below. Even a few words can help another reader
decide if the book is right for them.

http://www.Amazon.com/gp/customer-reviews/write-a-r
eview.html?asin=B085BXBB11

Join me online at www.priscillabakerauthor.com

***

Continue to the next page for Ally's famous seafood cioppino recipe and cooking techniques!

Ally's Seafood Cioppino

¼ cup olive oil
1 large fennel bulb, thinly sliced
1 onion, chopped
3 large shallots, chopped
2 teaspoons salt
5 large garlic cloves, finely chopped
3/4 teaspoon dried crushed red pepper flakes, plus more to taste

1/4 cup tomato paste
1 (28-ounce) can diced tomatoes in juice
1 1/2 cups dry white wine
5 cups fish stock
1 bay leaf
1 teaspoon paprika
1 pound mussels, scrubbed, debearded
1 pound uncooked large shrimp, peeled and deveined
1 1/2 pounds halibut
Fresh basil, chiffonade

Step 1: Add the olive oil to a large pot over medium heat. Add in the onion, shallot, and fennel. Cook for 3-5 minutes, until the ingredients have turned translucent and begun to brown. Add in the garlic and the crushed red pepper flakes and cook for another 3-5 minutes. Add one teaspoon of salt.

Step 2: Add the tomato paste, mixing well to blend with the onion mixture. Allow the paste to brown for a moment over the heat, but don't let it burn. Add in the white wine and use it to deglaze the pan, allowing it to release the browned fond from the bottom. This adds a delicious depth of flavor to the final product.

Step 3: Once the white wine has cooked off, add in the diced tomatoes, fish stock, bay leaf, and paprika. Stir to combine and allow to simmer over a low flame.

Step 4: While the stew simmers, add the seafood. Allow to cook until the shrimp have turned pink, the halibut flakes easily, and the mussels have opened completely. Discard any mussels that do not open. Salt and pepper to taste.

Step 5: Ladle in bowls and top with a basil chiffonade - serve with lots of fresh bread!

Technique: Basil Chiffonade
A chiffonade is a technique used to prepare herbs to be used as a garnish. The chiffonade is achieved by laying several clean leaves of the herb in question on top of each other, then rolling them lengthwise into a cigar shape. Using a sharp knife, slice the tube into thin ribbons, moving from one end to the other. This

will result in thin strips of the herb, perfect for garnishing.